DISNEP
fairies

Please Don't Feed the Tiger Lily!

By Tennant Redbank

Illustrated by Denise Shimabukuro
and the Disney Storybook Artists

Random House 🏠 New York

Dear Parent:

Congratulations! Your child is taking the first steps on an exciting journey. The destination? Independent reading!

STEP INTO READING® will help your child get there. The program offers five steps to reading success. Each step includes fun stories and colorful art. There are also Step into Reading Sticker Books, Step into Reading Math Readers, Step into Reading Phonics Readers, Step into Reading Write-In Readers, and Step into Reading Phonics Boxed Sets—a complete literacy program with something to interest every child.

Learning to Read, Step by Step!

Ready to Read   Preschool–Kindergarten
• big type and easy words • rhyme and rhythm • picture clues
For children who know the alphabet and are eager to begin reading.

Reading with Help   Preschool–Grade 1
• basic vocabulary • short sentences • simple stories
For children who recognize familiar words and sound out new words with help.

Reading on Your Own   Grades 1–3
• engaging characters • easy-to-follow plots • popular topics
For children who are ready to read on their own.

Reading Paragraphs   Grades 2–3
• challenging vocabulary • short paragraphs • exciting stories
For newly independent readers who read simple sentences with confidence.

Ready for Chapters   Grades 2–4
• chapters • longer paragraphs • full-color art
For children who want to take the plunge into chapter books but still like colorful pictures.

STEP INTO READING® is designed to give every child a successful reading experience. The grade levels are only guides. Children can progress through the steps at their own speed, developing confidence in their reading, no matter what their grade.

Remember, a lifetime love of reading starts with a single step!

For my amazing editor,
Liz Rudnick—T.R.

Copyright © 2011 Disney Enterprises, Inc. All rights reserved. Published in the United States by Random House Children's Books, a division of Random House, Inc., 1745 Broadway, New York, NY 10019, and in Canada by Random House of Canada Limited, Toronto, in conjunction with Disney Enterprises, Inc.

Step into Reading, Random House, and the Random House colophon are registered trademarks of Random House, Inc.

Visit us on the Web!
StepIntoReading.com
www.randomhouse.com/kids

Educators and librarians, for a variety of teaching tools, visit us at
www.randomhouse.com/teachers

Library of Congress Cataloging-in-Publication Data
Redbank, Tennant.
Please don't feed the tiger lily! / by Tennant Redbank ; illustrated by Denise Shimabukuro and the Disney Storybook Artists. — 1st ed.
p. cm. — (Disney fairies) (Step into reading. Step 3)
ISBN 978-0-7364-8090-1 (trade) — ISBN 978-0-7364-2750-0 (lib. bdg.)
I. Shimabukuro, Denise, ill. II. Disney Storybook Artists. III. Title. IV. Title: Please do not feed the tiger lily!
PZ7.R24455Pl 2011 [E]—dc22 2010008930

Printed in the United States of America   10 9 8 7 6 5 4 3 2

Lily flew to her garden.

She was a garden-talent fairy.

She could not wait

to see her newest flower.

She had planted it

four days earlier.

Three days earlier,

it had sprouted.

Two days earlier,

it had started growing.

One day earlier,

a bud had formed.

Today that bud was open!

Lily rushed over.

"Oh, tiger lily!"

she said to the plant.

"You are lovely!"

The tiger lily was bright orange

with dark stripes.

Lily splashed fresh water

on the ground

around the plant.

Snap! Snap! Snap!
The flower nipped
at Lily's fingers!

Just then, Iris flew by.

She spotted the tiger lily.

"Oh, Lily, you love every plant,

don't you?" Iris said.

"Tiger lilies can be

nasty flowers."

Lily blushed to her wingtips.

Iris held up her plant book.

She showed Lily the page

about tiger lilies.

"Be careful what you feed it,"

Iris warned Lily.

"No fairy food!"

The tiger lily snapped at Iris.

Iris backed away.

Then she flew off,

shaking her head.

Lily did not care.

She liked her flower.

She would tame the tiger lily!

"You're not bad,"

Lily said to the tiger lily.

The tiger lily grabbed

the sun hat off Lily's head.

Crunch, crunch, crunch.

In no time at all,

the hat was gone.

Lily laughed.

Iris was right.

She had to be careful.

She would build a fence

around her new plant.

Lily went to the beach

and found some driftwood.

She borrowed a hammer and nails from Tinker Bell.

Then Lily got to work.

She even made a sign.

It said: PLEASE DON'T FEED

THE TIGER LILY!

Lily nailed the sign

to the fence.

The tiger lily looked

at the sign.

The tiger lily growled.

The next morning,

Lily visited the tiger lily.

She talked to it for an hour.

She gave it water.

She made sure it had sunshine.

The tiger lily smiled at her.

"It's as sweet as sugarcane,"
Lily said.

PLEASE DON'T FEED the TIGER LILY!

But after lunch,

the tiger lily was not sweet.

It nipped at a dandelion.

Lily zipped over

to the tiger lily.

"Stop that!"

she scolded the plant.

Lily was puzzled.

The tiger lily was acting

as if it had eaten fairy food.

But she had not given it any.

So Lily just tried harder.

She gave the tiger lily

more water.

She talked and sang to it.

She asked a light-talent fairy

to give it extra light.

But the tiger lily did not
get any sweeter.
It barked at a dogwood.

It hissed at the cattails.

None of the flowers in Lily's garden
wanted to be near the tiger lily.

Lily tried and tried.

But the tiger lily

just got worse.

It scared off

a messenger fairy.

Lily left a rake

by the fence.

The tiger lily broke it in two.

Why was the flower

acting so mean?

One morning,

Lily had to collect seeds

in a faraway meadow.

She would be gone all day.

Lily was worried.

Would the tiger lily

be all right?

"Be good,"

she told the tiger lily.

The plant purred.

At the end of the day,

Lily went back to her garden.

She could not believe her eyes.

The tiger lily was huge!

"Tiger lily!"
Lily cried.
"You're so big!"
She flew over to it.
This time,
the tiger lily did not purr.
It roared!

Lily jumped back.

How had it gotten so big?

And why was it so grouchy?

Then Lily spotted nutshells

inside the fence.

She saw crumbs.

She found peapods

and a sour-plum pit.

Someone had been feeding

her tiger lily!

Lily raced to the Home Tree.
She burst into the tearoom.
"Who fed my tiger lily?"
she cried.

She put her hands on her hips
and looked around the room.
Bess turned pale.
Tink gulped.
Prilla, Rani, and Beck slid down
in their chairs.

Only Vidia looked at Lily.

"I did," she said.

She flipped her dark ponytail.

"Vidia!" Lily yelled.

"You fed my tiger lily.

And now it's grouchy!"

Tink flew between Lily and Vidia.

"It's not all Vidia's fault,"

she said.

"I fed your flower, too."

Then Bess came forward.

"Me too,"

she said.

Rani, Prilla, and Beck

got up from their chairs.

"And me,"

each fairy said

at the same time.

Lily's glow lost its angry color.

She sat down.

"You all fed my tiger lily?"

she asked.

"Why?"

Tink put her arm around Lily.

"Come on," Tink said.

"We'll show you."

Tink flew ahead.

Lily and the other fairies

followed.

Lily ducked

behind a yellow poppy.

Beck hid

behind a tulip.

Prilla, Rani, and Bess sneaked

into some lilacs.

Tink put a finger to her lips.

"Shhh," she said.

"Don't let the tiger lily

see you!"

Lily nodded.

Then Tink flew up to the plant.

Lily could not believe her eyes.

The tiger lily drooped

against the fence.

It looked sad!

It looked hungry!

But Lily knew the tiger lily
wasn't sad.

It wasn't hungry, either.

Lily darted forward.

"You sneaky little flower!"
she said.

"You're so clever,
you fooled everyone!"

The tiger lily hung its head.

The sign reads:

PLEASE
DON'T FEED
the
TIGER
LILY!

Then Lily turned
to her fairy friends.
She pointed to the sign.
"From now on," she said,
"please don't feed the tiger lily!"

The other fairies listened
to Lily.
They didn't feed the tiger lily.
Day after day,
Lily gave the flower only water
and sunshine.

Soon the tiger lily really was
as sweet as sugarcane . . .
most of the time.